FEIWEL AND FRIENDS NEW YORK

I LOVE YOU MORE THAN . . .

written by
TAYE DIGGS

illustrated by
SHANE W. EVANS

My child.

I am not always with you as much as I'd like.

and chilling
inside my heart.

These are the
times I like
to think about
how much . . .

I LOVE YOU.

But I love making
up moves and
moonwalking with you

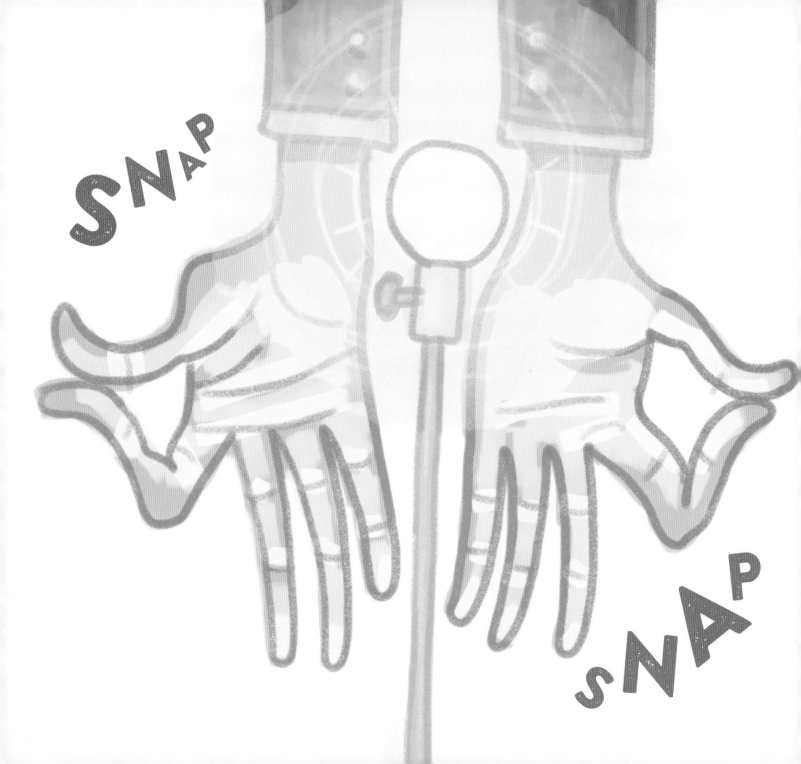

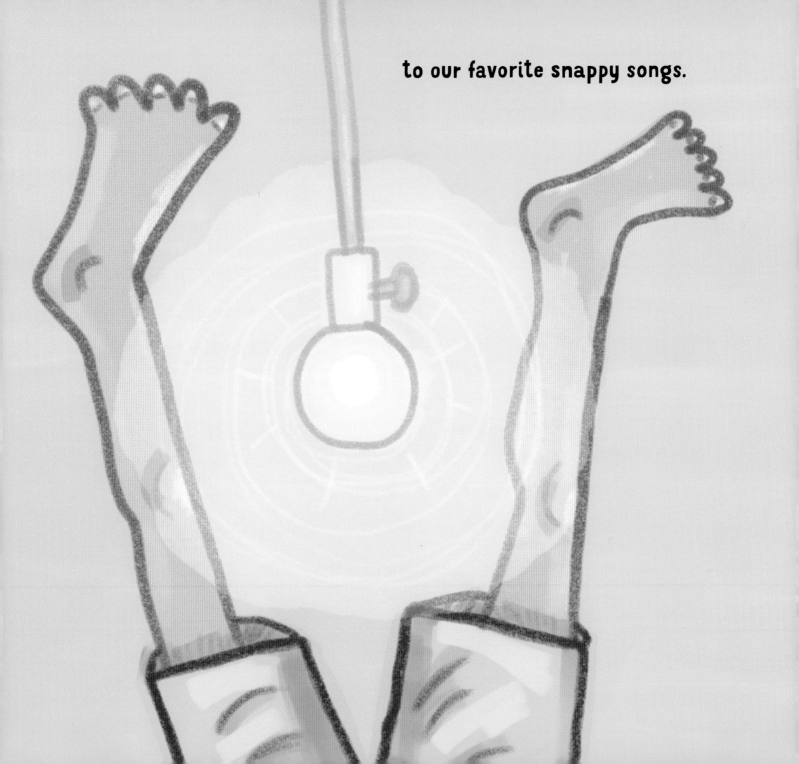

to our favorite snappy songs.

I love you more
than I love
singing. . . .

But I love to belt out
your favorite
la la la lullaby

before you
fall asleep.

I love you more than I love going to the movies.... But I love how you look in those 3-D glasses

when we check out a booming big-space action flick.

I love you more than I love
the beach. . . .
But I love the
footprints your little feet
make when I'm chasing
you through the sand.

I love you more than I love eating.... But I love going to breakfast with you. We get pounds of pancakes and apple juice. (Sometimes I'll mix the juice with water so it's not so sweet.)

YOU CAN EAT
Nuts
Banana
Chips

ALL DAY CAKES
Blueberr
Apple
Raisin

Seeds

Plum

Pear

I love you more than all my sneakers....

But I love how you look in your cool little kicks. They make you run so super fast.

I love you more than
New York City....

But I love riding
the subway with
you and taking our
time talking on our
way to school.

I love you more than
so many things.

I love you more
than everything.

I JUST LOVE YOU.

YOU!

I dedicate this book to Walker and to all families who long to see
each other more often. You are loved more than . . .

—T.D.

Thank God for the gift of creative life, for the gift of this work and
for the Sun . . . for the Child. This book is dedicated to my brother, Robert,
and my daughter, Yurie . . . Always thinking of you.

—S.W.E.

A FEIWEL AND FRIENDS BOOK
An imprint of Macmillan Publishing Group, LLC
175 Fifth Avenue, New York, NY 10010

I LOVE YOU MORE THAN . . . Text copyright © 2018 by Taye Diggs. Illustrations copyright © 2018 by Shane W. Evans.
All rights reserved. Printed in China by RR Donnelley Asia Printing Solutions Ltd., Dongguan City, Guangdong Province.

Our books may be purchased in bulk for promotional, educational, or business use. Please contact your local bookseller or the
Macmillan Corporate and Premium Sales Department at (800) 221-7945 ext. 5442 or by e-mail at MacmillanSpecialMarkets@macmillan.com.

Library of Congress Cataloging-in-Publication Data is available.
ISBN 978-1-250-13534-6 (hardcover)

Book design by Carol Ly
Feiwel and Friends logo designed by Filomena Tuosto
First edition, 2018

The artwork was created with mixed media: ink, alkyd resins, digital resources, and, of course, love.

1 3 5 7 9 10 8 6 4 2

mackids.com